CANDLEWICK PRESS

Dedicated to the actors, artists, and experts who brought this story to life.

Cast: Anthony, Cody, Doug, Eliza, Ivy, Margot, Michelle, Mohini & Veda
Photographers: Jess & Stewart
Studio Assistants: Lei & Nick
Train Expert: Bill

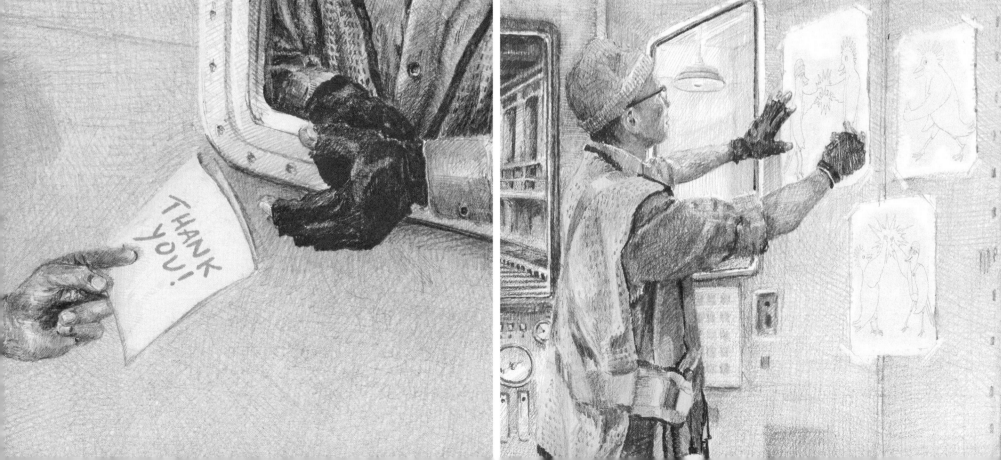